BEN M. BA

The Brave Bunny

Illustrated by
Andy Ellis

A
LITTLE APPLE
PAPERBACK

SCHOLASTIC INC.
New York Toronto London Auckland Sydney
Mexico City New Delhi Hong Kong Buenos Aires

ISBN 0-439-41917-4

Text copyright © 2001 by Working Partners Limited.
Original series created by Ben M. Baglio.
Illustrations copyright © 2001 by Andy Ellis.

12 11 10 9 8 7   4 5 6 7 8/0

Printed in the U.S.A.   40
First Scholastic printing, March 2003

To Tabitha and Hannah

Special thanks to Linda Chapman

1

"Don't forget to take your reading books home with you, class!" called Ms. Rushton, Mandy Hope's third-grade teacher. "I'll see you all on Monday."

Mandy grabbed her bag and pulled on her coat. "Have a nice weekend, Ms. Rushton!" she called as she followed her friends out onto the playground.

"Mandy! Over here!"

Mandy's grandpa was standing next to Mr. Baker, whose daughter, Laura, was in first grade.

Mandy ran over to them.

"Hello, Grandpa," she said. "How come you're here to pick me up?"

"Your mom's had to go up to Giant's Farm," her grandpa explained. "One of Mr. Grove's cows is ill. And your dad's at the animal sanctuary."

Mandy nodded. Her mom and dad were both vets. They often had to leave their clinic, Animal Ark, to visit sick animals.

Just then, Laura Baker came charging across the playground, her dark curly hair bouncing. "Hi, Dad!" she cried, flinging herself into Mr. Baker's arms. She swung around. "Hi, Mandy!"

Mr. Baker smiled. "Mandy's grandpa's just been giving me

some advice on growing
vegetables, Laura. He's offered to
come and take a look at my
lettuces."

"What? Now?" Laura asked.
When her father nodded, she
looked very excited. "You can

come and see Nibbles, my new rabbit, Mandy!" she said.

"What color is he?" Mandy asked. She loved rabbits.

"Black and white," Laura told her, her eyes shining. "He's really cute. But he's only four months old and a little shy."

Mr. Baker shook his head. "Laura's rabbit crazy," he said. "I hope you don't mind talking about rabbits all the way home, Mandy!"

Mandy grinned. She couldn't think of anything nicer. "Oh, no, I *love* talking about animals!" she said.

2

When they reached the Bakers'
house, Mr. Baker took them
through the wooden side gate into
the backyard. Mr. Baker and
Grandpa headed toward the
vegetable patch.

Laura took Mandy's hand
and pulled her toward the back of
the yard. "Come and see Nibbles!"
she said. She led Mandy to a large
wooden hutch.

Mandy crouched down.
Behind the wire mesh was a
young black-and-white rabbit.

He sat back and looked at
Mandy with bright, dark eyes. His
whiskers wobbled nervously. Then
slowly, he hopped over and stood
up on his hind legs to say hello.

"He's sweet!" Mandy said softly. She reached out a finger and gently tickled Nibbles through the wire.

Laura nodded happily. "He seems to like you," she said. "You can hold him, if you like." She opened the hutch and lifted Nibbles out.

Mandy took the young rabbit from Laura's arms. She was careful to support his back legs, just like her mom and dad had shown her.

Nibbles cuddled in close. "Oh, he's really gorgeous!" Mandy said, feeling his soft fur and the quick patter of his heartbeat. "Why did you name him Nibbles?"

"Because he nibbles
everything!" Laura said with a
laugh. "His food, treats,
bedding — he even nibbles at his
cage and water bottle."

Just then, the back door of the
house opened and a small boy

came running out into the yard. "Laura!" he shouted. "Auntie Katie said you were home from school!"

"Tom!" Laura said in surprise, as the little boy ran toward them. "What are you doing here?"

"Mommy and I came for dinner," Tom said.

Laura turned to Mandy. "Tom's my cousin," she explained. "He's three."

Mandy smiled at the little boy. He had a round face and dark curls just like Laura. "Hi, Tom. I'm Mandy," she said.

But Tom wasn't listening. He was staring at Nibbles. "Can I hold your bunny, Laura? Can I? Please? Can I hold him?" he asked eagerly. "Can I? Please?"

"No, Tom," Laura said quickly. "You're too little. You'll drop him."

"I won't, I promise!" Tom said loudly.

Nibbles squirmed in Mandy's arms. "Tom, you're frightening Nibbles," she said gently. "He's only a baby — he doesn't like loud noises."

"*Sorry!*" Tom whispered.

"Maybe you should just pet him, Tom," Laura said.

"But I want to *hold* him." Tom looked like he was about to cry.

"Well . . ." said Laura, frowning a little doubtfully. "Maybe you could just hold him for a *few* seconds."

"Oh, yes, please!" Tom whispered.

Laura took Nibbles from Mandy. "You must be really

careful," she said as she handed him to Tom. "You mustn't let him go."

The little boy took the rabbit into his arms. For a moment, he stood there, beaming, but then Nibbles began to wriggle.

"Ooh! That tickles!" He laughed, forgetting to be quiet.

Frightened, Nibbles wriggled more. Tom tried to hang on to the struggling bunny. But he just couldn't keep hold. With one last kick, Nibbles twisted himself out of Tom's grasp and leaped to the ground!

3

"Nibbles!" Laura cried in alarm.

Mandy moved quickly. She threw herself onto the grass and grabbed Nibbles.

The frightened bunny struggled, his sharp claws catching on Mandy's bare arms.

Mandy sat up and pulled him close to her chest. She knew Nibbles didn't mean to hurt her. "It's OK, Nibbles," she soothed.

"Oh, Mandy!" Laura cried, dropping onto the grass beside her. "Is he all right?"

"He's fine," Mandy said, as she felt Nibbles settle in her arms.

"I didn't mean to drop him, Laura!" Tom gulped, tears welling in his eyes.

Mandy saw Laura frown and

spoke quickly. "We know you didn't mean it, Tom," she said. "You were just so excited."

Tom nodded.

"Would you like to pet Nibbles while I hold him?" Mandy asked him.

"Yes, please," Tom whispered. Crouching down beside Mandy, he patted Nibbles very carefully. "I'm sorry, Laura," he said, looking up at his cousin.

Laura seemed to forgive him. She sighed. "That's all right. I should have known you were too little to hold him."

She took her rabbit from Mandy and put him in his run. Nibbles shook himself for a

moment and then hopped off
happily across the grass.

"I wish I had a bunny,"
Tom said, as Nibbles turned and
looked at them, his black nose
twitching.

Just then, they heard the
sound of the back door opening.

Mrs. Baker, Laura's mom, came out. "Dinner!" she called.

Mandy followed Laura and Tom inside. Her grandpa and Mr. Baker were in the kitchen with Mrs. Baker and Tom's mom.

"Mrs. Baker's invited us to stay for a light dinner," Grandpa said to Mandy.

"Can we take ours upstairs, Mom?" Laura asked. "I want to show Mandy my bedroom."

"All right," Mrs. Baker agreed.

Tom turned to his mom. "Can I take mine outside?" he asked.

His mom nodded. "Yes, but don't feed your sandwich to Nibbles," she warned him.

Tom's eyes widened. "I wouldn't, Mommy!"

Mandy and Laura went upstairs with their sandwiches and cake.

"My room's just been decorated," Laura said to Mandy. "Look!" She pushed open her bedroom door.

Mandy gasped. The room was covered with rabbits! There were rabbits on the wallpaper, rabbits on the curtains, rabbits on Laura's blanket — even the light shade had a rabbit on it! "Wow!" she exclaimed. "You must *really* like rabbits, Laura. I've never seen so many!"

"Isn't it wonderful?" Laura

said happily. She put her plate
down and picked up a photo
frame from her bedside table.
"Look, this is Nibbles the day we
got him."

Mandy looked at the picture
of Nibbles. He looked cuter than
ever, snuggled deep in Laura's
arms, his bright eyes sparkling at
the camera.

"I can see his hutch from my window," Laura said. She went to the window and looked out. "What's Tom doing?" she asked with a sudden frown.

Mandy joined her. Tom wasn't eating his meal. He was running around the yard below, laughing happily. He seemed to be chasing something.

At exactly the same moment, Mandy and Laura gasped. Hopping along in front of Tom was Nibbles!

4

Mandy and Laura raced downstairs. The grown-ups had moved into the living room. Not stopping to get them, the two girls ran outside.

"Oh, Mandy! Nibbles will escape!" Laura panted.

Nibbles was hopping around near the fence at the back of the yard. He looked like he was having a wonderful time. Every few hops, he would pause and nibble at a piece of grass or a nearby bush.

Tom ran along behind him, laughing.

"Tom!" Laura shouted, racing across the yard.

The little boy swung around. The smile left his face as he saw his angry cousin.

"What are you doing?" Laura cried.

Seeing Nibbles begin to hop straight toward a gap in the fence, Mandy sped up. She raced over, reaching the fence just before Nibbles did. The black-and-white rabbit stopped and looked at her.

"Come here, Nibbles," Mandy said, crouching down. But with a nervous flick of his ears, Nibbles turned and hopped away across the lawn.

"Don't chase him!" Mandy said, seeing Laura and Tom about to run after him. "He might panic even

more!" Laura and Tom stopped
and looked at her. "Let's try and
close in on him quietly," Mandy
told them.

Seeing that they had stopped,
Nibbles paused, too, and began to
nibble at a patch of buttercups.
He kept a wary eye on them, his
ears flickering as they began to
creep toward him.

"Come here, Nibbles," Laura said softly. But as they got close, Nibbles bounded away again. "We'll never catch him!" she cried.

"Are there any treats that he really likes?" Mandy asked. "Some carrots or cabbage or something? Maybe then we could get him to come to us."

"He loves dried apple pieces," Laura said. "I'll go and get some!"

Leaving Mandy and Tom to make sure that Nibbles didn't escape from the yard, Laura ran into the house.

She returned a few minutes later with a bag of dried apple slices. "Here," she said, pushing the bag into Mandy's hand.

"OK," said Mandy, her eyes glued on the little rabbit. "Let's creep up very slowly. When we get near, I'll try and get close to him using these."

They began to move in on Nibbles. He looked around at them.

"Here we are, Nibbles," Mandy called softly. She crouched down and held out a piece of apple. "Look what I've got!"

At first, she thought the bunny was going to run away again. But suddenly, his nose twitched as he caught the scent of his favorite treat. Slowly, he hopped toward Mandy.

Mandy waited until he was
very close to her and then
dropped the piece of apple on the
ground.

As Nibbles bent down to snatch it in his teeth, Mandy flung herself down and grabbed him. "Got you!" she said softly.

Laura and Tom ran over.
"Oh, Nibbles!" Laura said. "It's naughty to run away like that!"

A yellow buttercup petal quivered on Nibbles's nose. He didn't look very naughty. In fact, he looked quite relieved to be safe in Mandy's arms!

Mandy grinned and wiped the petal away. "I think it's time you went back in your hutch," she said to the little rabbit. "That's enough adventure for one day!"

Back at Animal Ark that evening, Mandy told her mom and dad all about Nibbles and his trip around Laura's yard.

"Well, at least it all ended happily!" Dr. Emily said with a laugh.

"For Nibbles, anyway," said Mandy. "Laura's cousin got told off!"

Just then, the phone rang.

"I'll get it," Dr. Adam said. He got up from his armchair and went into the hall.

Mandy watched her dad through the doorway as he picked up the receiver.

"Animal Ark — Adam Hope speaking," he said.

There was a pause, then Mandy saw a serious look cross her dad's face. "Of course, Mr. Baker," he said quickly. "Bring

34

him here now and I'll take a look at him."

"Mr. Baker?" Mandy said, as her dad put the phone down. "Was that Laura's dad?"

Mr. Hope nodded, with a serious look on his face. "Laura and her father are bringing Nibbles to Animal Ark right away, Mandy. He sounds very sick."

5

Although it was nearly Mandy's bedtime, her mom said that she could stay up and wait for Mr. Baker to arrive.

Fifteen minutes later, there was a knock on the front door.

Dr. Adam let Mr. Baker and Laura in. Mr. Baker was holding a cardboard box. "I'm sorry about calling so late," he said.

Laura clung to her dad's side.

Her face was pale and she looked as if she had been crying.

"Bring Nibbles into the examination room," Dr. Adam said gently. "Let's have a look at him."

"Can I come, too, Dad?" Mandy asked.

Her dad nodded, and she followed Laura and Mr. Baker into the clinic.

Mr. Baker put the box down on the examination table and took Nibbles out. The poor little rabbit sat in a huddled heap. His ears were flat and his eyes half closed. He was trembling, too.

Mandy swallowed. Nibbles looked really sick!

Dr. Adam stroked the rabbit.
"So when did you notice that
something was the matter?" he
asked.

"Just over an hour ago," Mr.
Baker replied. "Laura went out to
check on him."

"He was sitting all hunched up in a corner of his hutch," Laura said. "He didn't want to play or eat anything."

She looked at Nibbles, her eyes filling with tears. "I told Dad and he said that we should leave him for a while to see if he got better. But he didn't get better, and now he's got an upset tummy."

Laura's dad gave her a hug.

"It sounds as though he might have eaten something that disagreed with him," Dr. Adam said thoughtfully. "Can you think of anything in the yard that might be poisonous — poppies, foxgloves, buttercups . . ."

"Buttercups!" Mandy gasped before Mr. Baker or Laura could say a word. She remembered the yellow petal on Nibbles's nose. "He did eat some buttercups, Dad!"

Laura nodded. "Yes, I remember!"

"I didn't realize buttercups were poisonous," said Mr. Baker, surprised.

"They're very poisonous to rabbits," Dr. Adam said seriously. "If Nibbles has eaten some, then he's going to be feeling very bad." He turned to Laura. "I think Nibbles will have to stay here for a while, Laura."

Laura's lower lip wobbled and she clutched her dad's hand.

"But first, I'll give him a little injection to help stop his tummy from hurting," said Dr. Adam kindly. "Then we'll go and settle him down in one of the cages. He's too sick to drink, so I'll put him on a drip."

"Will that hurt him?" Laura whispered.

"Not at all," Dr. Adam said. He gave Nibbles a quick injection, then picked him up. "Now, shall we go and make him comfortable for the night?"

Laura nodded. They all went into the residential unit. Animals that were too sick to go home stayed there.

Dr. Adam settled Nibbles in
one of the rabbit cages. He put a
heating pad under him to keep
him warm. Then he fixed a drip to
one of Nibbles's ears.

"I think we should leave him
alone now," he said. "Nibbles will
need all his strength to get well.
Let's see how he is in the
morning."

6

Mandy found it hard to sleep that night. All she could think about was Nibbles. What if he didn't get better?

As soon as she heard her parents start to get up, she jumped out of bed and ran into their room.

"Mandy!" her mom said, looking around in surprise. "What's wrong?"

"Can we go and see how Nibbles is?" Mandy asked, looking at her dad.

"It's very early," Dr. Adam said.

"Please!" Mandy pleaded.

Dr. Adam looked at Mandy's worried face and nodded. "All right," he said. Pulling on his bathrobe, he followed Mandy downstairs.

Nibbles was lying in his cage. He wasn't hunched up like he had been the night before, but he didn't look very well. He was still trembling a little.

Dr. Adam opened the cage door and checked Nibbles over.

"Oh, Dad," Mandy said. "He is going to get better, isn't he?"

"I did warn you that he's really not very well, Mandy," Dr. Adam said quietly. He ran his hands over the rabbit's coat. "I've given him all the medicine I can. Now, it's up to him. He has to fight to get better." He closed the door of the cage.

"Can I stay with him, Dad?" Mandy asked.

"Not now, dear," Dr. Adam said. "Let him rest a little more. Come back and see him after breakfast."

When Mandy returned, Nibbles was still lying quietly on his blanket. She stared at him through the wire front of the cage. "Oh, Nibbles, you've *got* to be brave!" she whispered. She opened the cage door and petted him gently.

The little rabbit opened his eyes. For a moment his nose twitched. Mandy had the feeling that being stroked comforted him, so she continued.

After a while, her dad came in. "I just got a phone call from the Bakers," he said. "They're going to come around later to see Nibbles."

Dr. Adam looked in the cage. "He's looking a little better," he said.

Mandy looked closely. Nibbles still wasn't moving. But his eyes did look brighter, and he had stopped trembling. "I've been petting him," she told her dad.

"Well, keep it up," Dr. Adam said, smiling. "Nibbles seems to be liking it." Then he went to start Animal Ark's Saturday morning rounds.

Mandy kept petting Nibbles and talking softly to him.

Soon, the door to the residential unit opened. Her dad came in with Laura and Mr. Baker. A tearstained Tom was with them, too. The little boy was clutching a bag of apple pieces.

"Nibbles!" Laura cried,
running over to the cage.

At the sound of Laura's voice,
Mandy saw Nibbles's ears twitch.
He raised his head a little and saw
his owner. His nose wobbled once.
Then he made a huge effort and
hopped bravely to the front of the
cage.

"Well!" said Dr. Adam, looking very surprised. "That's a good sign!"

"Oh, Nibbles," Laura whispered.

The little rabbit nudged his black nose against the wire of the cage.

Laura tickled his face with her finger. "Does this mean he's going to get better, Dr. Adam?" she asked.

"It certainly looks like it," Mandy's dad replied. "He must be a very brave bunny, Laura. I didn't expect him to make such a quick recovery!" He opened the cage door and gently handed Nibbles to his owner.

Mandy felt so happy as she looked at Laura cuddling Nibbles. Everyone was smiling.

"Can I take him home now?" Laura asked.

"I think it might be best if he stays here for one more night," said Dr. Adam. "Just to make sure he's completely recovered."

Laura looked disappointed but she nodded.

Tom pulled on Mr. Baker's hand. "Can I give Nibbles a piece of apple, Uncle Peter?" he whispered shyly.

Mr. Baker looked at Dr. Adam. "Would that be all right?"

"His tummy may still be feeling sore," Dr. Adam said to the

little boy. "He might not want it.
But you can try."

Mr. Baker lifted Tom up to
Nibbles's cage. "I'm sorry you've
been sick, Nibbles," he said
quietly.

The rabbit's nose twitched. Slowly, he reached out and took the piece of apple from Tom.

Dr. Adam grinned. "Yes, he's certainly feeling better!"

The next day, Mr. Baker, Laura, and Tom came to take Nibbles home. Mandy went with them. Laura carried Nibbles in his cardboard box.

"I've pulled up all the buttercups," Mr. Baker said, as they walked down the yard. He looked at Tom. "And I've mended the hole in the fence, so that even if Nibbles does get out, he should be safe," he added.

"But I won't *ever* let Nibbles out again without asking you, Laura," Tom said seriously.

"I know, Tom," said Laura, smiling at her cousin.

She looked up at her dad. "Can I let Nibbles have a quick run around the yard now, please?" she begged. "I know it would cheer him up!"

Mr. Baker laughed. "Well, I suppose that would be all right," he said. "He can't get into much trouble now."

Laura put down the box and lifted Nibbles out onto the grass.

The little rabbit looked around a little. He twitched his nose and flicked his ears. Then he began to hop across the lawn.

Everyone smiled as they saw the little rabbit hop away.

But suddenly, Mr. Baker didn't look very pleased. "He's heading for my lettuces!" he cried.

Nibbles had reached the vegetable patch. He looked boldly at Mr. Baker and then took a great

big nibble out of the nearest
lettuce.

Laura ran after Nibbles and
scooped him up.

Mandy laughed. "It looks like
Nibbles really *is* better now!" she
said.